To Chuck and John: Pirogues and sailboats.
Thanks for the contrast.

STERLING CHILDREN'S BOOKS
New York

An Imprint of Sterling Publishing Co., Inc.
1166 Avenue of the Americas
New York, NY 10036

ISBN 978-1-4549-2125-7

Distributed in Canada by Sterling Publishing
c/o Canadian Manda Group, 664 Annette Street
Toronto, Ontario, Canada M6S 2C8
Distributed in the United Kingdom by GMC Distribution Services
Castle Place, 166 High Street, Lewes, East Sussex, England BN7 1XU
Distributed in Australia by NewSouth Books, 45 Beach Street, Coogee, NSW 2034, Australia

For information about custom editions, special sales, and premium and corporate purchases, please contact
Sterling Special Sales at 800-805-5489 or specialsales@sterlingpublishing.com.

Manufactured in China
Lot #:
2 4 6 8 10 9 7 5 3 1
01/17

www.sterlingpublishing.com

Design by Irene Vandervoort

The artwork for this book was created in pastels on sanded paper.

HOOT & HONK
Just Can't Sleep

BY LESLIE HELAKOSKI

STERLING CHILDREN'S BOOKS
New York

HOOT & HONK
Just Can't Sleep

Grasses sway.

Storms rumble.

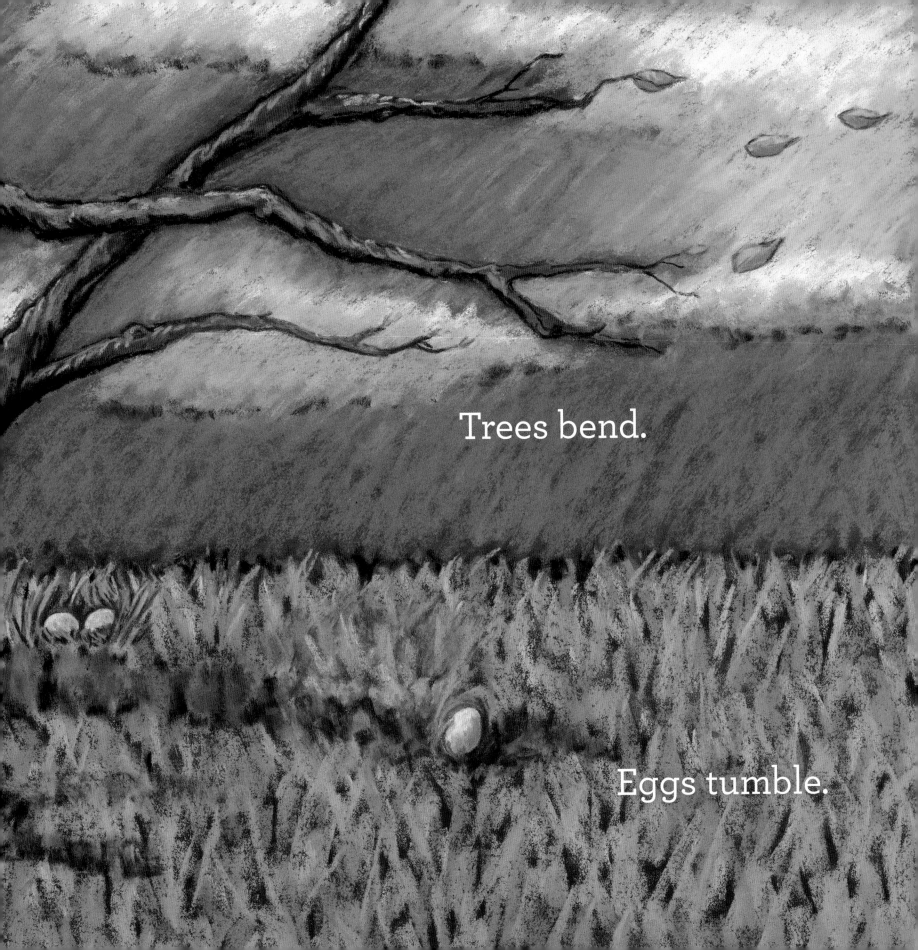

Trees bend.

Eggs tumble.

Hoot hatches.

Odd chick.

Bugs and seeds for dinner?

Ick!

Bedtime?

Dark skies.

Can't sleep.

Open eyes.

Scritch . . . Scratch . . . Scuttle . . . Splash!

Just. Can't. Sleep.

Who's up?

Moonlight.
Other chicks like the night!

Flap. Fly.

Shhh. Spy.

Not one sound.

Soar. Swoop.

Swallow. HOOT.

Owlet found!

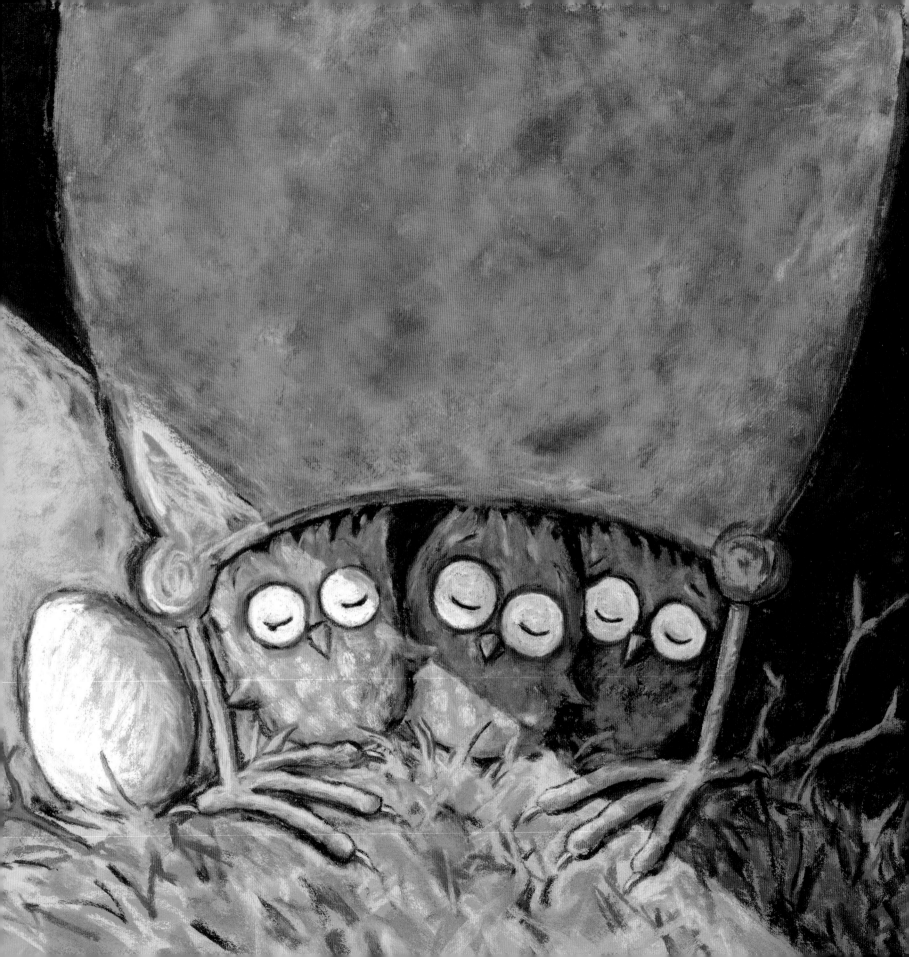

Sunrise.

Sleepy head.

Snuggled safely.

Home in bed.

Honk hatches.

Odd chick.

Fur and bones for dinner?

Ick!

Bedtime.

Light skies.

Can't sleep.

Open eyes.

Caw . . .   Moo . . . 'Doodle doo!

Just.
Can't.
Sleep.

Who's up?

So bright!

Other chicks like the light!

Wade. Wonk. Waddle. HONK.

Upside down.

Dip. Dunk. Oops. Kerplunk!

Gosling found!

Sunset.

Sleepy head.

Snuggled safely.

Home in bed.

Night and day.

Wake or doze?

Some eyes open.

Some eyes close.